Hotwife Affair In Lockdown - A Hotwife Multiple Partner Wife Watching Romance Novel

Karly Violet

Published by Karly Violet, 2021.

This is a work of fiction. Similarities to real people, places, or events are entirely coincidental.

HOTWIFE AFFAIR IN LOCKDOWN - A HOTWIFE MULTIPLE PARTNER WIFE WATCHING ROMANCE NOVEL

First edition. June 21, 2021.

Copyright © 2021 Karly Violet.

ISBN: 979-8201844332

Written by Karly Violet.

Hotwife Affair In Lockdown
A Hotwife Multiple Partner Wife Watching Romance Novel

Chapter One: The Layover

I'm tired of sitting in London, England. I'm tired of not seeing my wife for three long weeks and I'm tired of getting the runaround whenever I call the corporate office and beg for a way out of here. "No way we can do it," I snarl as I repeat the last thing Lydia from human resources said before hanging up on me. Of course, she'll claim that the connection from here to the east coast of the United States was a bad one and that it suddenly cut out, but I know she was actually getting tired of talking to me about the whole fucking situation.

"Hello?" I hear my groggy wife say on the other end of the FaceTime call. It's almost midnight there, but I want to hear her voice and see her beautiful face.

"Hey, baby," I say as I try to smile at her. "How are things on your end of the big pond?"

She smiles sweetly at me as she moves around in our bed to make herself more comfortable. "I guess they're okay, considering. How about for you?"

Shaking my head, I reply, "They tell me at corporate that I'm stuck here for at least another two or three weeks. That is, if this virus thing ends up being just a big misconception." COVID-19, as Sky News here in Britain has been calling it, is spreading across the world like wildfire. Though just weeks ago it was thought to be contained in China and some other parts of Asia, it has hit the coasts of the United States as well as parts of Europe and people are scared. There are just too many variables to this thing that are unknown, and people by and large have a problem with the unknown.

"I'm sorry, Leyland. I wish you hadn't gone on that trip in the first place."

"Five million dollars," I tell her. "That's why I'm supposedly here. The Brits were going to buy all kinds of aluminum pressed parts for a new assembly plant here. Though we had a deal a couple of weeks back, I'm not sure that's still in play at all. And now they won't let me the fuck out of this country." I'm tired of beans on toast and some of the other edible fare the hotel boasts. Sure, it was an interesting novelty to begin with, but it's now become a bit of an aggravating factor in my confinement here. The city leaders in London don't even want people on the streets until they know for certain what the hell this new virus is going to do.

"Maybe they'll find a way out of there for you yet, baby. Just have a little faith."

I shake my head. "It's not very likely. The news says that both countries are buttoned up pretty tightly. They aren't letting anyone in or out in either direction. Even if I could find a plane to return on, the U.S. side might put me into an indefinite quarantine at the airport." Though I have considered that at least being on United States soil might be a step in the right direction, the thought of having to sleep on a seat or floor in an airport waiting area doesn't sit well with me. At least here, I have a comfortable room in a decent hotel with all of the amenities.

"What can I do on this side?" Karie asks as she rubs her eyes.

"I don't know. Do you know any well-connected lawyers who could make a call to the U.S. government to get me out of here? Maybe one that has worked with some high-up official at one time?" My wife has been a criminal defense attorney for the last several years and in that time has become somewhat of a recognizable face among her own kind. Karie is an intelligent legal practitioner who could likely convince any jury that a serial murderer is in fact a misunderstood choir boy.

She laughs. "I know a few well-connected people, but they've all shot me down about this already. Short of you getting in contact with the U.S. Embassy there and having them help you, I'm afraid you're stuck for now."

"Fuck," I mutter as I shake my head. "There's one guy at the embassy..."

"Yeah, you know that won't work." My connection to the U.S. embassy in London is one that is tenuous at best. I've decided to hold back from talking to my wife's old boyfriend from college. There are still some hard feelings concerning the fact that I married Karie and he did not.

"So, what do we do?" I ask her. "I miss you, sweet muffin." My cock gets hard as I ask her, "Can I see your sweet muffin right now?"

My wife giggles while shaking her head. "You are a man with a one-track mind, aren't you? All those text messages that you sent me today kept vibrating my phone while I was on speaker phone for a court hearing. I think the judge suspected that I had a vibrator and was using it."

I laugh hard at the thought of what the judge's face might have looked like. "And that would have been a bad thing? I think it would have been great if you had used one on yourself while on the call."

"It would have been a terrible idea," Karie chuckles. "Anyway, here you go, my love. This is just for you and just because you are so far from home." My wife moves her phone down to the covers as she pulls them back. Just as she always does, Karie has been sleeping nude. She opens her legs for me to see the gentle curvature of her well-trimmed biscuit. I pull my cock out and begin to play with it as I sit back in my bed.

"Damn, baby," I say as I pull up on my johnson and cause a small drop of pre-come to ooze from my pisshole. "I can't believe you are so sexy."

She turns the phone back to her face and asks, "What are you doing over there, Leyland? Let me see." I switch the camera from front to back so that I can see her face while my wife is watching me rub my dick. "Are we really going to do this? While we are nearly four thousand miles away from each other?" Karie giggles as she turns her camera so that I can see her playing with her pussy. It's getting wet as she moves her fingers in and out of her soft vagina before running them over her swelling clitoris.

"Yeah. Let's come together," I plead with her as I pull hard on my fleshy rod. It won't take me long to pop this time. I haven't had my wife's soft hands on my cock in nearly a month and I'm getting tired of watching porn on my laptop and simply jerking off. Even though she can't touch me here, it turns me on that she can see me playing with myself. Of course, watching her do the same to herself helps me immeasurably as well.

"Leyland, you dirty man," she laughs as she fingers her wet hole. I watch as two of her fingers plunge deep into her pussy before she slowly pulls them out, apparently rubbing along her G-spot as she does.

"That's it," I groan as I continue to pre-come into my hand. I take some of the slippery natural lubricant and run it over the head of my penis with my fingers. My body aches to release as I think about how tight and soft Karie is inside her sweet pecan. "Fuck, I wish I was putting your legs back and tasting of you right now."

My wife pulls her fingers out of her twat and then follows them with the camera to her face. She smiles before sliding the wet digits into her mouth. She then slowly pulls them out and looks at me in the camera. "I'm sweet, Leyland. Very sweet. I might be ovulating right now." Karie laughs as she finishes licking and sucking off the wetness that is all over her fingers.

"You fucking little tease," I laugh as she moves the camera back to her cunt. She continues to finger and play with herself as her pelvis rocks back and forth on top of the bed. It won't be very long now. Karie orgasms easily as it is, and we have been going at this for several minutes at this point.

"Come for me, alright? Come hard for me when you do," she pleads with me. "Come all over yourself and the bed, Leyland. Make sure that you have the camera close enough so that I can see it spurt." Karie gets very horny at the sight of me coming hard. She has a special way of pulling up on my cock when I'm coming just to be certain that I spurt a longer distance. Using her thumb, she simply draws it up the underside of my meat as I begin to ejaculate into her hand. It does the trick, causing me to shoot my wad sometimes three of four feet into the air. If only she were here now to do that for me. I miss that sensation now that we are so far away from each other.

"I'll come hard," I promise her. "I want to hear you, okay? Be loud, baby." I love to hear my wife squeal as she releases and goes into an orgasm. She often tries to keep things lower key because we do have neighbors nearby. Karie has come to believe that she might be loud enough for them to hear her cry out during sex.

"Yes, come hard." Her fingers move faster. "I'm close, Leyland. Really close." Her hips are still rocking as she twirls her little missus between her puffy labia. "Damn, I don't think I can wait any longer."

"I'm about to lose it," I reply as I take short breaths. "Fuck, you need to tell me when I can go," I tell her. "Please just say when I can let go, honey."

"WHEN!!!" Karie's body suddenly shudders as she orgasms with her fingers deep inside her pussy. *"Fuck!!! Oh, FUCKKKK!!!"* Her hips twist around on the bed as she continues to play with her sweet folds and her swollen ladybit. *"Uhhh...OHHHH!!!"* My wife bites her lower lip as she spurts a little from her pussy. *"SHIT!!! FUCK!!!"* Her squeals are loud and sharp as her eyes close and she fully releases herself to enjoy the intense orgasm she is having.

"Nahhhh!!!" I begin to spurt and some of my semen lands on my cell phone before another spurt propels some onto my stomach and legs. *"Uhhh...ohhh...uhhh...ohhh..."* Squeezing my pecker hard, I run my hand up and down it as I milk myself. Though I don't have my wife here to help me, I seem to be doing a great job of getting as much spunk out of my balls as possible. *"Dammit...oh..."* Karie opens her eyes and smiles as she watches me come in front of the camera. We both enjoy seeing the other get off like this. It doesn't matter that we are so far away from each other.

"Shit...Leyland..." My beautiful blonde wife begins to slow her rocking on the bed as she pulls her fingers out of her vagina. They are covered with a lot of her own juices, which is one of the sure signs that she is probably ovulating right now. I feel a little jealous as I shake my head and laugh at the sight of us both. Karie moves the camera back up to her face.

"You are such a fucking tease," I tell her again. "I wish I could have been there to taste that and then to fuck you really hard. Karie, you are a hot little fox." We both laugh as I move the video back to my front-facing camera.

"So are you. I want to have sixty-nine when you get back, alright?" My wife offers a huge smile and I can't help but to pull on my wilted cock as I think about her proposition.

"Yeah, that would be awesome," I reply. "The problem is, I have to make it home first. Once I cross that hurdle, I'll toss your fucking salad, too."

Karie giggles. "Is that a promise?"

"You bet your tight asshole it is!" We both laugh as I look around the hotel room. I have enjoyed visiting England, but I'm ready to be back home. Being separated from Karie has been a real pain in the ass and a serious blow to my sex life. I've been tempted to hire an escort here, but the fact is I'm not sure whether something like that would be a serious offense if I'm caught. Besides, the authorities are threatening huge fines and other penalties here if someone is caught fraternizing with those not from their own household. I don't need to get myself into legal trouble while I'm in a foreign country.

"It's going to work out, Leyland. Just give it a little more time."

I nod my head. "Hopefully you're right." I allow one last smile before saying to her, "Have a restful night, my love. I'll talk to you later."

"I love you, baby."

"I love you, too." I leave the FaceTime session and sit back in my bed as my cock continues to slowly ooze jism all over my stomach. All I can do at this point is hope that my company comes through on their promise to get me back home soon. Otherwise, I might not see Karie for several more weeks yet. Three weeks has been enough time away from her. I want to be home right now.

Chapter Two: A Way Home

Goosebumps rise along my neck and shoulders as I step into the large Gulfstream private jet. As I turn to the right to make my way to a seat, I'm met by Ronnie Sykes, a man I knew well from college. A man who once yearned for the affection of my wife before I met her but never got it.

"Hey, do you have everything that you need?" he asks as he looks over and smiles at me. Ronnie takes my hand and shakes it as he directs me to a seat next to where he will be sitting.

"Yeah, I'm good," I tell him nervously. "Are you sure they won't shoot us down as we try to fly out of here?"

He chuckles. "Well, it would make a huge diplomatic stink if they were to shoot down a U.S. chartered diplomatic jet, wouldn't it?" We sit down as I nod my head and smile. It's been almost six weeks now since I left my wife in the States and I'm excited to get back to see her. Although, I am still worried that something could happen to stop the flight just before takeoff.

"We're clear to go, right?"

"Absolutely. The State Department has made certain to clear things on both sides of the pond. You will be home with Karie in just a few hours." Ronnie smiles, though I know behind that facade he would still like to punch me in the nose for taking her from him. At least, that's the way he took it when Karie and I began to date during our senior year at the university. They had talked a few times and even dated once or twice, but nothing ever got beyond a kiss. There was never any sexual relationship between the two of them, which is why my wife has never understood why Ronnie felt so strongly about their relationship or even the lack of one.

"That's good to hear. You know, I can't thank you enough for this ride. My company hasn't been very helpful at all in getting me back home."

He nods his head. "It's really not their fault, Leyland. The lockdowns are pretty stringent now that the coronavirus has spread throughout parts of both countries. As a matter of fact, we will land in Alexandria instead of Washington, D.C. because of the spiking numbers along the coast. As long as we go straight to our cars and leave the airport for our homes, we will be fine. After that, it's right back to the lockdown." The diplomatic aide seems to be taking things in stride as he talks about the restrictions that have been put into place to try to slow or stop the spread of the new virus. I wish I could be as confident as he that things will be alright.

"Still, they left me high and dry. They shouldn't have sent me after the Chinese admitted that the virus was there. Anyone with any sense could see that it wasn't a good time for international travel."

"You're right," he replies. "Just keep in mind that this thing has blown up in our faces, Leyland. I think the Chinese government was probably keeping a lot from us in the beginning."

"And probably still." Ronnie nods his head. If anyone should know how these things go, he should. I sigh. "It'll be so nice to be back in my own bed." Looking over at him, I ask, "And what about your wife? What's her name again?"

Ronnie looks down at his cell phone as if checking a message before replying, "Michelle is her name and she's not exactly enthusiastic about me coming home soon."

"What do you mean?" I watch the expression on his face change a little as he shakes his head.

"Well, that means that my new home is an apartment in D.C. for the time being. Michelle is busy entertaining someone else at this time."

"What?" I sit back in my seat and buckle my seatbelt as I hear the captain's voice in the intercom.

"We are now taxiing toward our runway. Please fasten your seatbelts and keep drinks put away until we are in the air. There is a flight attendant available to help you with whatever you need once we have gained altitude to forty thousand feet. Have a nice flight." The announcement ends and I watch the flight attendant walk past us, his eyes looking at our seatbelts before moving on to the rest of the six passengers on the airplane.

"I hate flying," Ronnie tells me as he sits back in his seat. He doesn't look out through the window beside me as the Gulfstream lines up on its runway and then begins to pick up speed.

"Yeah, I'm not a fan, either," I admit as the aircraft begins to lift from the asphalt below. We watch as Heathrow Airport quickly drops below us and the jet flies quickly toward the clouds above.

"Five or six hours if we're lucky," Ronnie mutters as he stares straight ahead. In just minutes the plane levels out and an announcement from the cockpit lets us know that we can unfasten our belts if we would like. Neither Ronnie or I do so as we continue our earlier conversation.

"Why in D.C.?" I ask him as I try to move our conversation along.

He laughs a bit. "Michelle has a new friend that she doesn't want me to know about." Shaking his head, Ronnie continues, "She's been having an affair for some time and I found out recently that it's become a real hot one. This guy is from the Pentagon and while I've been out of the country they've been hitting the sheets together." His eyes glance over into mine for a moment before turning away. "So, I've decided that I should stay in D.C. until that simmers down a little."

I raise an eyebrow as I try to understand what he's telling me. "Wait. Does she know that you know about the boyfriend?"

Ronnie looks over at me. "We haven't had that conversation just yet," he replies dryly. "Maybe eventually I'll broach the subject, but not now."

"You can't be serious," I say as I shake my head. "You're just going to let her keep seeing this guy?"

"That's the plan. At least, for now." The diplomatic aide seems relatively content with his decision to allow Michelle to continue with the other man. This strikes me as completely odd as I think about what would happen if such a thing occurred in my own marriage.

"Why?"

Ronnie shrugs his shoulders. "I don't know. I guess it's because I just want to save my marriage." He can see the confusion on my face, so he adds, "I love Michelle, Leyland. I don't want to do anything to change the fact that I'm married to an incredible woman who I know loves me back. That's something that's really important in a relationship."

"What's important in a relationship is honesty and loyalty," I reply as I shake my head. "I can't see how this is going to be helpful for either of you in the long term. I mean, if you go home then she will have to give this up, right? It would make it too hard for her."

"That's why I'm staying away from home for a couple of weeks. I've told her it's to make sure that I'm not carrying the virus to her."

"Shit, man."

"Look, you don't understand. Michelle and I have a very special relationship with each other."

My jaw drops before saying, "There is no way I would let Karie do that to me, Ronnie. There would be hell to pay, at least for the man she was seeing."

Ronnie's blue eyes lock onto mine. "I know what it's like to lose a woman to another man, Leyland. This time I'm going to do whatever I can to keep my wife." I get by the look on his face that he is referring to the near-relationship he had with Karie before I met her. There are still some hard feelings on his side of things, which is why my wife didn't want me to contact him in the first place. I was just completely out of options with my own company, though. Getting home has become so important to me that I was willing to take a chance that Ronnie might simply tell me to screw myself. Besides, I haven't told Karie that I am coming home just yet. I hope to surprise her.

"I get it," I finally respond. "It's just a little weird, you know? Most guys wouldn't like knowing that their wives are cheating on them."

"I don't like it," he retorts. "And yeah, it's weird. But what else can I do? If I give Michelle some ultimatum to quit what she's doing with that guy, she might just decide to choose him and leave me. Then what? I'll be back to being alone. I don't like the feeling of that, Leyland." Again, it seems that Ronnie is trying to use our past experiences to grind on me just a little. I can't blame him, though. Karie is an awesome woman and wife. I'm so relieved that I will never have to worry about her doing what his wife is doing behind his back right now.

"I hope it works out," I tell him as I smile and nod my head. "I really do." My phone buzzes and I pull it out of my shirt pocket. A text message has only just now come in from Karie as I am leaving England. There doesn't appear to be enough signal to respond, so I just read it.

"I want to have another FaceTime session tomorrow, alright? Just text and tell me when." A couple of lips and hearts adorn the message on my phone.

Putting it away, I tell Ronnie, "I think I'll hit the head. I'll be back in a few."

"Yeah, I'll get you a drink for when you get back." He smiles at me as I get up and begin to make my way to the lavatory at the back of the aircraft. What Ronnie has told me about Michelle was a huge surprise. The thought of her rocking some other man's world behind Ronnie's back has to be eating at him.

"I'm so glad that I have Karie," I say to myself as I enter the lavatory and close the door behind me. Very glad indeed.

Chapter Three: Welcoming Arms

"Leyland!" Karie is surprised to see me after opening the front door of our home. "You're *here?*"

"I'm home, honey." I reach out and take my wife into my arms, embracing her tightly as I inhale her sweet perfume. It's been almost six weeks since we have last been so close together and I can barely contain myself as I feel her soft face next to mine.

"But, how?" She shakes her head as we let go of each other and I close the door behind me. "I thought they wouldn't be able to get you out for at least another month." Her brown eyes focus hard on me as she crosses her arms. I feel as if she is somehow disappointed to see me.

"Well, I know you didn't want me to reach out to him, but Ronnie Sykes was a huge help. As a matter of fact, we both flew home on the same government jet." I smile widely as I watch the surprise in Karie's face.

"That's good. Really good." She pulls out her cell phone and says, "Just give me a moment, alright? I'm supposed to text Leesa back. She'll be excited to know that you have gotten home." My wife nods her head and turns to walk toward the dining room. I put my suitcase down on the floor beside the door and then look at the recliner waiting for me nearby. It doesn't take me long to reacquaint myself with my favorite piece of furniture in the living room.

"It's good to be home," I say quietly as I run my hands along the worn leather of the old seat.

"Okay, um, what now?" Karie asks as she comes back into the living room a couple of minutes later. "Is the company closed down?"

"For now," I reply with a grimace. "They say that they're going to pay us through May, but I'm not sure they will be able to do that. I called in to tell them that I found another ride home and they didn't seem all that concerned about it. It was strange, really. I would expect some of the people I know to be happier about me being back in the States." Though I attempt to make this sound like a commentary on the way my own employer has dropped the ball on getting me home, I am also dumbfounded as to why Karie appears less than ecstatic at my arrival. For my part, I feel as if I could bounce off the walls after finally getting to see her again. That doesn't seem to be the case for her.

"We're shuttered at the firm as well," Karie informs me as she sits down in a chair nearby. "As for pay, we are going to get this month's normal salary, but after that it's all up in the air. The partners are hoping that this thing doesn't last all that long."

"But it could," I reply. "From what Ronnie told me during the flight, the government is ratcheting up for a months-long or even a years-long scenario. It's scary, to be honest." The new virus has everyone talking about what has happened or could happen in the near future.

"Two weeks, some have said. Just to flatten the curve."

I shake my head. "It's not what the government really thinks if Ronnie is correct." I have my doubts that things will be back to normal soon. Still, getting to come home finally is a huge relief to me.

"So, how's Ronnie doing?" Karie asks as she looks over at me. "Is he doing okay?"

"I guess he's as okay as he can be," I reply. "His wife, Michelle, is having an affair behind his back, but he seems to be taking things in stride."

My wife sits back in her chair and looks down at her hands before saying, "Sometimes people do stupid things, I guess."

"Yeah, I guess so." As I look at her, I can see that Karie has become a little distant for a moment. "Is everything alright, baby? I know I should have called before just dropping right at the front door, but I thought you would be happy to see me."

She looks over and smiles at me. "Oh, Leyland, I'm extremely happy to see you." Karie gets up from her chair and walks over to me. She bends over and puts her hands on my face, pulling me to her so that our mouths meet. The kiss is sincere and sweet, causing my heart to patter hard as I once again catch a whiff of her perfume. I love this woman. She is everything I have ever wanted in a wife and then some.

Karie smiles at me before going back to her chair and sitting down. "Is he going to divorce her?"

"His wife?" She nods her head at the stupid question. "No. As a matter of fact, he says he will probably just stay at a place in Washington, D.C. for a while longer to let her get her dalliance finished up before he goes home.

"What?" Karie laughs a little. "I mean, *why?*"

"I don't know, honestly. I asked him that same question and he said that he loved her too much and couldn't bear to lose her. I'm guessing he's still trying to process all that he's found out about her over the last few weeks. It doesn't seem like a healthy marriage."

"The cheating part?"

"And probably some other things, but yeah, the cheating part." I smile at Karie and add, "At least I know where we stand. I would hate to be dragged into that kind of nightmare."

"That would be a terrible thing, huh?" My wife shakes her head and looks away for a moment before turning her attention back to me. "Do you think that she might leave him instead? Is her affair all that serious?"

"There's no way I could know that," I say with a grimace. "Still, it's got to be a shot in the gut for the guy. Ronnie all but used that situation to bring back up what happened between the three of us in college."

Karie's eyes widen for a moment. "Do you think he's still upset about that?"

I shrug my shoulders. "Probably. I mean, I don't know for certain, but he seemed to push the idea that I'm still to blame for his problems."

"He said that?"

"Not in so many words," I admit. "It's just a feeling that I had while talking to him. Ronnie wasn't very happy with us back then and I doubt that he's changed his mind much about that. You were his boyfriend, after all," I add while grinning.

"We were *not* together like that," Karie answers indignantly. "We only went out a couple of times and we almost didn't kiss. I wasn't going to kiss him on that second date, but he leaned in and I didn't have any choice."

"Of course you didn't," I chuckle while shaking my head.

"Leyland, don't." This is a sore point for not just Ronnie, but for my wife as well. It took Ronnie Sykes the better part of a year to stop calling Karie even though it was obvious that we had become serious. He had a terrible problem letting go and apparently thought there was a lot more to their relationship than just a couple of very casual dates.

"I'm sorry. It just sucks for him, that's all. He had found a great woman and then I swooped in and took her away. Then when he thought that he had found another, it turns out that she's screwing someone behind his back. That's got to really mess with someone's head."

"The cheating thing is hard, I guess. I wish things were better for him," she says as she looks down at her hands again. It's the sort of thing that Karie has always done whenever she goes deep into thought about something. I'm not sure what is bothering her, but I'm simply happy to be back home at this moment.

"We should make a nice dinner tonight. Do we have anything in the freezer that would be great to thaw and cook?"

"I bought some groceries on delivery," she replies. "There's chicken, beef, and even a couple of lamb chops. They aren't allowing more than twenty or so shoppers in the supermarket downtown. I tried to get inside on Tuesday afternoon, but there were too many people waiting to go in. I didn't even bother to get out of the car. It's easier to order things online and wait for them to show up."

"Yeah, I guess it would be," I reply. "So, I'll cook us some chicken?"

"Sure, that sounds good," Karie answers with a slight smile.

"And what else?"

"I don't know. You make whatever you want to make. I need to go lie down for a while. It's been a long day for me on the laptop while trying to figure out the new court schedule for the cases I have. Do you want me to help you first?"

"No, go ahead and lay down," I say to her. "Get some rest, Karie." Smiling, I stand from my recliner and offer my wife a hand. She takes it and gets up before turning and walking out of the living room toward the back of the house. My mind begins to work out what is going on with her.

"Just tired? That's not like her," I say to myself as I shake my head. "What's bothering you so much, honey?" After some thought, I begin to chalk up what I am seeing with her to the stress we are all feeling over the COVID-19 virus. There are just so many unknowns right now that none of us can be certain what will happen over the next few weeks. No one, except maybe the government. I've long thought them to know a great deal more than the general public on such things, and it worries me that this virus could be some new biological weapon. I've been told that I'm nuts for thinking such a thing, but how can someone not suspect those in power of screwing with Mother Nature? It wouldn't be the first time, and it certainly would not be the last.

Chapter Four: Too Many Coincidences

Trina Melton has been our next door neighbor for the last six years and has always had a kind word to say whenever she sees either of us outside. I smile as I walk over to the short hedge row that separates our back lawns.

"Good morning," I say as I smile at her. "I'm sorry if I don't come all the way to the edge of the yard. Social distancing and all, right?"

The forty-something woman nods her head. "I hate that term already, but I'm afraid it's here for a while," she replies. "You found a way home, huh?"

"Yes I did. Thanks to a guy I know who was stationed at the U.S. embassy in London. If it hadn't been for him, I might have been stuck there for the next several months."

"Uh, that would have been a drag." The woman, a divorcee for the last few years, shakes her head full of dark brown hair. Trina is an attractive MILF, about five-six and maybe one-twenty soaking wet. She's been known to enjoy the company of a few younger men now and again, though Karie and I don't ask her about her social life when we see her.

"How have things been for you over the last few weeks?" I ask.

Trina shrugs her shoulders and replies, "Everything is fine here. My ex-husband has to pay me a monthly allowance and it's more than enough to survive on. I hate that my hair salon employees won't be getting a check for a while, though."

"It's going to be tough all the way around," I reply. "Those damned politicians don't know what the hell they're doing. If they're not careful, we're all going to die from that virus."

"Maybe," Trina answers with a chuckle. "I'm a pretty tough woman, though. It will have to work me over really well to end me."

"Hopefully that's true for most of us." I smile as I look back at my own house. Karie is still in bed and asleep after a long night of looking over some of her assigned case files. Though she likely won't be able to go to court for the next few weeks, she is still persistent in her work for her clients.

"I have noticed over the last few weeks that there have been visitors to your house, especially early on Saturday mornings. You might want to be careful of that. The health department officials are saying that family members should stay in their own households for now to slow the spread of the virus."

"Visitors? We don't have family anywhere near here," I reply. "Except for Karie's sister, who lives about a hundred miles away."

"Really?" Trina raises an eyebrow. "But there have been cars here on and off. Especially on Saturday mornings. I just assumed that it was family." Again, I turn and look at the house. My mind begins to spin with possibilities of who could have come to our home over the last few weeks. I turn to look back at our neighbor as she offers, "Maybe it's some of her clients?"

I nod my head. "They could be. I know Karie is worried that things will get backed up in court and she's hoping to at least be able to attend some hearings over video. She's not heard from any of the judges on her cases yet, though."

Trina sighs. "Things are too screwed up right now."

"What did the people who came over to my house look like?" I ask.

"Well, most of them were young guys, maybe in their twenties. I saw one who might pass as in his mid-thirties. It's hard to tell from my house, though. They didn't look like felons, though. Wouldn't they look a little rougher if they were involved in a court case?"

I laugh. "Not necessarily. Some of her visitors might have been other attorneys from her law firm. Karie has had them over here before."

"Ah, that makes sense. Most of the cars were nicer. That must be it, then. She's seeing her colleagues from the firm." Trina nods her head as if she's trying to convince herself of what we are saying. What does she really think? That my wife is doing something unseemly with all of those visitors? That's not the sort of thing Karie would ever involve herself in, especially with neighbors nearby who are constantly keeping an eye on everything that goes on in the neighborhood.

"How's Jake?" I ask as I change the subject to her eighteen-year-old son. "He's in his first year of college, right? At Georgetown?"

Trina smiles widely. "He has a full-ride. I'm thankful that my ex gave our son some of his intelligence. It's hard to believe, though, with all that he did behind my back. Did you know that Shane was having sex with other men?"

"Um, yeah, I think you told me that before. I'm sorry that happened to you."

"Another woman I could understand. I get that. But a *guy?* What does that say about me? Was I not good enough to keep him straight?" Trina shakes her head as she fumbles at her jacket pocket. "Oh, I forgot. I quit last month."

"Smoking?" She nods her head. "Good for you."

"I guess so. Sometimes I just need one good drag, though." She smiles at me, her green eyes focusing on me for a bit too long for comfort. If I were a betting man, I would bet that Trina would bed me in a heartbeat if I was of the same mind. The thing is, it wouldn't take much for her to get me into bed if I thought I could get away with it. Trina is a beautiful, sexy woman. Unfortunately, she's also a very stubborn and arrogant person in general. It is probably one reason that her husband decided to have an affair.

"Keep up with what happens in your own home, Leyland. You should know how things can fall apart so quickly. Don't let that happen to you."

"You mean the people visiting my house? I don't think Karie would let them come over if they had any of the virus symptoms."

"Maybe not. Still, be aware of who is visiting your house. You never know when one of them might be after something that you have." Trina smiles and adds, "I think I have a couple of cigs in the pantry inside. I might just take a puff or two for old time's sake. Have a good day, Leyland."

"You too." I watch as she walks back to her house and goes inside. Pressing my lips together, I look down at the hedge in front of me and admire the straight edges the gardener left on his last visit. There will likely not be another visit for some time, though, and I can't help but feel some sympathy for the fact that he will be losing practically all of his income during the coronavirus threat.

"Men here at my house," I say to myself as I look back at the patio and shake my head. I turn and make my way to a chair there and sit down as I look at the early morning sun. "Lance, Dyllon, and maybe Bert," I practically chant as I think of three of the five partners at the firm. I've seen them around here plenty of times, especially when Karie has an important case that will be coming before a judge soon. They are all likely planning their next moves for how they will handle their clients during this uncertain time.

"No, don't think that way," I tell myself. "Trina is always all talk, Leyland. Just ignore what she told you. Move on." I know my wife as well as I know myself. Karie is the sort of woman who dedicates herself to someone or something and stays the course. More than ten years ago we said *I do* to each other and we both take our vows very seriously.

"Damned law partners," I grumble. "When are you going to give her a shot?" Karie has been an attorney at the firm for the last six years and has won more cases there than any other attorney. She makes a lot of money for the firm, yet she hasn't been given any notice as to when she might be offered a partner role there. It irritates me to think of her putting in so much work during late evenings and weekends without even a hint of when they will consider her as their equal. After all, my wife could leave and find a position at any number of other law firms tomorrow if she really wanted. The pandemic wouldn't stop her from doing that.

"Hey, sweetie." I turn to see Karie walking out onto the patio. She makes her way to me and gives me a sweet kiss on the cheek before sitting down nearby. "I saw you chatting with Trina a few minutes ago. How's she doing today?"

I clear my throat. "She's good," I reply. "Her son is good too. She says he's enjoying college so far."

"That's great." Karie smiles as she leans back in her chair. "The breeze is really cool this morning, isn't it?" Her brown eyes glisten in the early morning sunlight as her blonde hair blows in the gentle breeze.

"It's nice. I just wish everything else was just as nice."

Karie smiles at me. "Don't worry about COVID, Ley. Things will get better soon and we can both be back at work. Have no fear."

"You're probably right." I consider for a moment whether I should bring up what Trina told me minutes ago. Should I ask about the men who have visited my wife here? No, I shouldn't. I know that they are likely law partners or other attorneys from her firm. I have no reason to suspect my beautiful wife of doing anything behind my back.

"I know I'm right. I'm the best attorney in the state, after all, right?"

I laugh with her. "You know, I think you probably are. Hopefully you will get the chance to have your cases heard soon, though."

"That would be nice. I miss everyone at work too." I feel goosebumps rise along the back of my neck. "I'm tired of just using FaceTime or Zoom to have our meetings. You know how Lance feels about getting sick. He's a little bit of a germaphobe."

"Yeah, I remember you saying something like that before." My heart races as I think about what Trina and my wife have both told me. What was going on at my house while I was away? Karie is essentially telling me that not one of her coworkers or the law partners have been over here recently.

"I'm going to make myself some coffee. Would you like a cup?"

"That would be great," I say while smiling over at her. I watch as Karie gets up from her chair and walks back into the house through the large French doors. Sitting back, I swallow hard and begin to take stock in what I know.

"Several different guys, one at a time with nice cars. They can't be her clients. Apparently none of them are Lance or the other partners. Who are they, then?" Baffled, I cross my arms and take a deep breath. I'm not going to ask my wife about these visitors just yet. Hopefully I'm simply overreacting to the piece of information Trina gave me. In all likelihood, Karie has been working hard to keep her clients happy. I have to trust that what has happened here has been related to that endeavor.

Chapter Five: A Startling Discovery

I can't sleep as I think about what Trina told me about the visitors to my house while I was in England. I want to believe that there was nothing nefarious going on, but I can't shake the feeling that Karie is hiding something from me. So, I get out of the bed quietly so as not to disturb my wife before making my way to the den. Once inside, I close the door and go have a seat at my desk. After opening up my laptop, I access our home security camera network and begin to look through some of the saved files.

"Saturday mornings," I mutter as I pull up the last several files from those times. All videos are kept on the hard drive of a central system in the event that someone breaks into the house and we need evidence for a prosecution. It was Karie's suggestion that I make sure we could collect good video evidence in the event something happened.

As I scan through the files and open them up, there is constantly something odd that I notice. "Where's the fucking video?" I ask as I pan through a six to ten o'clock in the morning file from three weeks ago. The file appears to be empty. "Shit." Shaking my head, I click on another Saturday morning file. It too, at about the same time, is blank. Convinced that there must be some sort of malfunction in the system, I check the other cameras from the same time. Nothing. Not one shred of saved video files from any of the cameras exist.

"What the hell is wrong with you?" I rhetorically ask the laptop on my desk. I move to yesterday's file, the last Saturday on the list, and check the same time slot. To my amazement, there is a video in this file which includes my brief conversation with Trina in the backyard as well as everything going on throughout the house. Why is this file available while several others are not?

Becoming concerned that something could have been tampered with in the system, I decide to check one last camera. This one is installed in our bedroom in a clock on the wall and Karie is not aware of its existence. The file from this camera is stored on a separate drive in my laptop and I can access it with a password. The purpose of the camera has been to record our fun together in the bedroom so that I could go back and jerk off to it later. It seems that this one is working as I click through and open the video box.

I fast-forward as I look at the images racing by on the screen. Then, a blur of something catches my eye. Moving the scroll bar back, I let the video play at normal speed and turn up the speaker on my laptop.

"It's too damned early," I hear a man say just before he walks into the video. "Can't we just meet later in the day?"

"Not here." I recognize my wife's voice as I sit back in my chair and watch the screen carefully. I grit my teeth together as I begin to wonder what is happening between her and the unknown man. He isn't someone I have seen before. "It's my neighbor."

"Ah, the one who likes to watch your house all the time?"

"She's up by eight o'clock almost every morning and stays up really late at night. I don't think she'll bother peeping too much earlier in the day, though. In the evenings, she sits on that front porch and watches everything happening in the neighborhood. It's gotten worse since the lockdowns began. There isn't a single soul in the neighborhood she doesn't know about."

The man laughs. "Well, that's a good thing, right? She makes sure that you don't have any criminal mischief going around."

"I guess so." Karie smiles warmly at him as she asks, "How are your cases working out? Will the judge hear them out soon?" Suddenly I am able to allow myself a quick sigh of relief.

"It's just work," I chuckle as I feel my face turning deep red. "Thank goodness, honey. You really had me going. And I'm going to have to fix the security system too." I almost close the laptop and put it toward the side, but then I see the man's hand extend toward Karie's arm. He takes hold of her and pulls her toward him. They immediately lock lips.

"Dammit, James," she says with a giggle as he moves to her neck and nibbles on it. "You are so persistent."

"I've wanted you for a long time," he replies. James is tall, maybe six feet, and his sandy blond hair is perfectly parted on the left side of his head. It's apparent through his polo shirt that he's a fitness buff as well, his muscular chest pulsating as he brings Karie's lips to his again.

"Dammit." I close my eyes for a moment as I think about what I am seeing. My wife, the one who I thought could never do any wrong by me, is a cheater. She's probably been seeing this guy for several weeks, and if it weren't for Trina I would have never known about it.

"Here, lie back," she says to him. James sits down on the edge of my bed before my wife kneels on the floor just in front of him. She reaches for his belt and begins to unfasten it before unzipping his pants. In seconds, Karie has the large, hard cock of the handsome man deep inside her mouth.

"Holy fuck, you are a natural," he says to her as he pulls her shoulder-length blonde hair to the side. "I knew that you could do this, Karie. Just talking to you I knew that you could give a guy a great hummer."

My wife lifts her head and looks at him. "I promised that I could deliver, right? Now I'm proving it to you." She goes back down and once again gobbles on his pecker.

"This is your first time with him," I say in disbelief. "Then who the hell else has been here?" The thought that Karie might have fucked several other men begins to enrage me. "Why would you do this to me? I've been faithful, dammit! Why are you seeing other men while I'm stuck in fucking London?" The opportunities I had to have an escort visit me in my hotel room come back to my mind. I didn't do such a thing simply because of my love for Karie and the promises we have made to each other. We were meant for each other, or so I have told myself for the last ten years. Yet here she is, sucking off another man as I watch.

My cock is getting hard as I see her massage his balls with her soft hands. James lies back and enjoys every lick, suck, and rub that he's getting from Karie. I can't really blame him for reacting this way with her. My wife is an astounding giver of oral sex. Any man would be lucky to have a woman like her give him a blow job like the one she is giving this guy in the video. Suddenly, I realize that Karie is likely the one who edited the video files on the main security system to erase her infidelity.

"Shit." I unzip my pants and pull out my cock as I watch it all happen before me. "You're cheating on me you little bitch," I groan as I pull hard on my manhood. I'm angry at the thought that Karie is cheating on me with another man, but there's a deep sense of lust that seems to be overwhelming that anger and jealousy. "Come in her mouth," I say to the man on the screen as I twist my hand around my stalk. "Come and choke her with it. Fuck, I want her to swallow it all."

"You're going to make me pop," James exclaims as he grips the edge of the bed with his hands tightly. My wife's head is bobbing up and down as she attempts to siphon his cock. "Holy shit, you're going to make me go over."

Karie stops and looks up at the man, a smile on her face. "Not yet, baby. Hang on." She pulls his pants down to the floor and slips them off over his feet along with his shoes. She then stands up and pulls her tee shirt off over her head before unfastening her bra to reveal her beautiful C-cup breasts. Her dark pink nipples are taut as she drops her shorts and thong underwear to reveal her soft, trimmed snatch. My wife straddles James and slowly lowers herself on top of him as her pussy takes in his large, throbbing pole.

"Damn, sweetpea," he says to her as Karie begins to move up and down, her labia tightly gripping his shaft. "No rubber?"

"I don't like them," she replies with a giggle. "It's not natural, and you told me that you like things as natural as possible, right?" She bends down and kisses him hard as his balls slap against her. James is now thrusting in unison with the rocking motion of my wife's pelvis. How good it must feel for him to bury so deeply inside Karie that he can most likely feel her cervix on the tip of his dick.

"I'm so grateful that you asked me to come over," he tells her as my wife sits up and begins to move herself up and down along his cock a little faster. "Your husband, though…"

"He won't know," she promises. Karie's fingers run around the outline of his nipples, causing them to stand erect. "Don't worry about anything, James. He's in England and will probably have to stay there for a long time."

"Lucky me," he chuckles as he reaches up and plays with her firm boobs. "All natural, huh?"

"Those too," she laughs. Their bodies begin to move even faster together as they enjoy fucking each other. "You rub me just right when I lean back, James." Karie leans back further and closes her eyes as she pulls on her own nipples. "I'm getting so close."

"Me too," he moans as he puts his hands on her thighs.

"Dammit, you cheating slut," I say through my teeth as I feel my balls begin to ache. I am trying to remain as quiet as possible since Karie is in the bedroom just down the hallway, but I'm finding it more and more difficult to do so as I watch her with another man in the video. "Fuck."

"Karie…" Her lover's eyes grow large. *"KARIE!!!"* He begins to come inside my wife's tight hole as she rocks hard on top of him. *"Fuck…"*

"UHHHHH!!!" Karie comes as well, her hips gyrating on top of James as she enjoys the feeling of his warm, salty semen spraying into her vagina. *"James…ohhhh…"*

"Ahhh…uhhh…uhhh…" He spurts over and over again, some of his white man gravy making its way out of my wife's tight muff. My breathing and heart rates quicken as I watch the two of them together.

"FUCK!!!" I suddenly begin to come hard as I pull on my cock with my right hand. Three powerful spurts have left the end of my pole before I realize that I'm making a mess all over my laptop. Turning my chair quickly, I continue to lose my wad into my hand and the floor in front of me. *"Motherfucker…dammit…Karie…"*

The two lovers on the video finish with each other just as I feel the last eruption of my jism from the end of my penis. I turn to watch them as they simply embrace each other with his dick inside my wife's pussy. They are finished and so am I. Reaching over, I close the video file and sit back in my desk chair. I hear something moving in the hallway just outside the den. The door suddenly opens.

"Leyland?" Karie says as she squints her eyes and looks inside from the doorway. "What are you doing in here?" I hide my wet manhood inside my shorts as I turn toward the desk.

"I'm just finishing up some work online," I lie. "The buyers in England were wanting some new specs on what we can provide once things ease up with the virus restrictions."

"Now? It's three in the morning. Shouldn't you be in bed?"

I nod my head as my nose suddenly catches the aroma of my jism on the keyboard of the laptop. Though I should probably close it, I know that if I do the wet slush from my balls might work its way inside and ruin the computer.

"I know it's a weird time to be up, but I just couldn't sleep. I won't be much longer, though. Just let me wrap things up in here."

"Alright," Karie replies with a soft smile on her face. "Come to bed and snuggle with me as soon as you can." My wife turns and leaves the den as my heart thumps hard inside my chest. At this moment, I am experiencing a myriad of feelings about Karie and what she has done while I was away. Not only did she decide to see at least one other man for sex, she also tried to keep this fact from me by wiping the incriminating evidence from the security camera footage. How long does she plan to keep this up? Is it over now that I'm back home?

"What will you do, Leyland?" I ask myself quietly as I begin to wipe off the laptop keyboard with a Kleenex. The fact that Karie has screwed around behind my back is one thing that I will have to deal with, but so is the way I handled it. Instead of getting up and marching into the bedroom to confront my wife, I sat and watched the entire thing unfold before my eyes while masturbating to the images. There came a point in the video when I wanted James to screw her hard. I wanted him to come inside Karie. There's no way to get around what has happened early this morning. My lust for seeing her with another man somehow outweighed my jealousy and anger over the entire betrayal. There are things I need to reckon with soon if I am going to figure out what to do about her visitors.

Chapter Six: Fulfilling a Need

I've thought about it all day long and decided that I can't just let things go as they are. I have to speak to Karie about what happened with James. I need to know if that was the only time that happened and if there are other men with whom she has had a fling or two. Sure, I could probably try to ignore it in much the same way Ronnie has ignored what his wife has been doing, but that doesn't sit very well with me.

"I need to talk to you," I tell her as I walk into the living room where Karie is sitting and working on her laptop. "It's pretty important."

"Oh, okay," she replies as she closes the laptop and puts it to the side. I sit down beside her on the sofa as I feel my body quivering from what I am about to say to her. How will Karie respond? Will she respond at all or will she just sit and stare at me?

"I don't know how to begin," I start off as I pull out my cell phone and grip it in my hand. "I guess I'll just begin by telling you that I know about him, Karie." My skin crawls as I look toward her from the side.

"I'm sorry, what?" My wife's brow raises as she looks intently at me. She doesn't understand yet where I am going with this.

After taking a deep breath, I tell her, "I know about James."

Her brown eyes do not flinch as she stares back at me. "James who? What are you talking about, Leyland?"

I shake my head as I look down at the cell phone in my hands. Have I made a mistake in bringing this up with her? Is Ronnie correct in his approach to how he is handling his own wife's cheating? Though I want to get up and walk away, I can't. No, I have to ask her about what she's been up to inside our home.

"I'll show you," I tell her as I unlock my phone and pull up the video file I have downloaded from my laptop. I start the video before handing the phone to my wife.

"What's this?"

"Just watch," I reply as I cross my arms and sit back in my seat. "It will explain everything." Taking a deep breath, I sit calmly and wait for

Karie to see what I have seen on the hidden security footage. It doesn't take long before she hands the phone back to me.

"I don't want this," she tells me. The expression on her face is stoic as she stares at the wall across the living room. Karie is undoubtedly trying to figure out how to answer for what she has seen on the video.

"How long has this been going on?" I finally ask calmly.

My wife doesn't answer immediately, but after a half-minute or so she replies, "I can explain this, Leyland. We don't have to make a huge fuss over anything."

I shake my head. "I haven't said that I'll make a fuss over what has happened. I just asked you a simple question. How long has this been going on?"

Her eyes turn for a moment to look into mine before she looks away again. "Leyland, I don't know what to say. It just happened."

"Not from what I've heard," I answer as I feel myself becoming mildly angry. "I've had a long talk with Trina. There have been men coming over here pretty regularly, especially on Saturday mornings. How long has this been going on?" It's the third time that I have asked the question, but I honestly want to know. I *deserve* to know. Why is she now trying to hide any of this from me since I know that she has been having sex with at least one other man?

"Trina is a busybody who lies, Leyland."

"So, she's lying to me about what she's seen going on over here while I was gone? Is that your argument?"

"No, I guess not, but it's just more complicated than that."

"Then tell me what you've been up to, honey. Was James just one of several other men?" I have no direct evidence of another man just yet. Though I was able to find the video of James with my wife, I haven't tried to look at any other hidden footage just yet. I haven't been able to bring myself to do so. At the moment, I am grateful for installing the camera in our bedroom the way that I did. Karie wasn't able to erase that footage.

Karie's face turns pale. "Leyland, please..."

"Just fucking tell me," I interrupt gruffly. "I already know that you've been up to something around here in our bed. All I'm asking is that you tell me the truth now. Can you at least do that much?" My heart beats hard inside my chest as I stare into my wife's dark brown eyes.

She takes a quick breath before answering, "There have been a few others." Karie shakes her head as she admits, "They are attorneys and others I have worked with over the years. Some of them have been sending me emails and text messages telling me how attractive I am and how they want to be with me. Some of them were just so convincing that I couldn't say no to them."

"Convincing? Do you mean that they were able to get you to cheat behind my back so easily?"

"I don't know what I mean," she retorts as her eyes fill with tears. "Leyland, you know that our sex life hasn't been all that exciting for a long time. Your trip to England just made things worse for me. After a couple of weeks, the emails and text messages seemed to come a lot more frequently and one thing led to another."

"Wow." Shaking my head, I get up from where I am sitting and begin to pace the floor in the living room. "I couldn't be here, Karie. It wasn't really my fault."

"I know it wasn't your fault. Still, you weren't here and I already needed someone to help me with the way I was feeling. I needed to feel a man's body beside me."

"And *inside* you," I say with some vulgarity. "Apparently a condom wasn't all that important to you, either."

"Leyland, that's not very fair."

"I didn't screw around with another woman while I was in London, Karie. I could have very easily, though. Did you know that there are escorts over there? I could have hired one or two of them and probably put it on the company's tab. Why am I so faithful to you while you fuck other guys behind my back?"

"I'm sorry," she replies while wiping her eyes. "If I had thought that you would find out about that, I would have..." Karie stops herself.

"Erased the video from that camera like you did all the others," I say as I finish the sentence for her.

Karie shakes her head. "Please, Leyland."

"Please doesn't really help anything," I reply coldly. "I know things were a little rocky in our sex life, but I thought we were getting better? We even went to see that therapist that you wanted to see."

"I know. There's just something that I felt like I needed that I haven't gotten from you in a long time."

"An itch you needed scratched." I turn away from my wife to face the wall for a moment. It's difficult to admit that maybe I haven't been the best lover for Karie. Then again, she's been a little cool to the touch as well sometimes. Still, we aren't a lost cause by any stretch of the imagination. We love each other deeply. I love her. Doesn't that count for something?

Karie sighs. "It happened. I can't change any of that," she tells me. "I wish I could. I would go back and stop myself from doing anything that would hurt you if I could. Leyland, I love you so much. None of what happened between me and the others was about love. I just needed to be with another man."

"Or men," I interject.

She nods her head. "Four others." My wife has finally answered my question to some degree. Karie has bedded four other men while I have been gone to England. I should be furious at this point, but I'm not. Instead, I'm only mildly irritated as well as a little sexually intrigued. Something is off about me and the way I am thinking about this whole thing.

"I watched the video and got hard," I admit. "I jerked off." Turning, I can see that my wife's brown eyes are focused squarely on me.

"You *masturbated?*"

"Yeah, I did. I shouldn't have. It was the other morning when you came into the den looking for me. I had just finished up watching and getting off. Why is that, Karie? Why am I upset about this but also so turned on by the whole thing? It's not right."

She gets up from where she is sitting and walks over to me. Putting a hand on my shoulder, she tells me, "I think you have the same problem that I have, sweetie. You want to have some new experiences too."

"I don't want other women."

"But you like knowing that I've been with other men, don't you?" Karie's hand slips down to the crotch of my pants. She can feel the raging hardon I have just behind the denim material. "You liked seeing me with James, didn't you?"

I almost stutter as I begin to answer, my mind uncertain as to how I should respond. "I liked it." Karie understands the quiet reply and smiles at me. I can't help but smile as well.

"Would you want to watch me with another man, Leyland? Would that make you happy?"

"Another man? Do you mean that you would want to fuck someone else again?"

"Only if you want me to," she replies. "Only if that's something that you would want. I will never do that again if you ask me not to. I've hurt you already." Karie smiles at me. Her sweet face causes my body to almost melt at the sight of her.

"Maybe." I can't believe that I'm agreeing to something so naughty. Why would I want my wife to fuck other men? I think I know why, but I'm having a hard time admitting to my own lusts and fantasies. I liked seeing James sink his long shaft into Karie's pussy. I want to see it again. I want to see other men doing that as well.

"We can do this as a couple," she tells me excitedly. "I don't mind if you watch, sweetie. You can watch me with every single one of them if you like." The excitement in Karie's voice is obvious as she discusses having sex with other men. Perhaps she understands the sexual satisfaction I got while masturbating to the video. It could be the same thing that drives her to have sex with them.

"I think I might want to try doing that," I tell her. "I'm a little scared of what that means, but I want to do it. Maybe only once, though, but we can talk about it afterward."

"Then you're okay with this?" Karie asks as she studies my face.

"For one time to start with, then we will talk some more about it." I swallow hard as my wife gives me a tight hug. I smile at her before we kiss and then her hand slips into my pants to play with my hard cock.

"Come to bed with me," she tells me with a giggle. "I'm going to rock your world, baby." I follow Karie to the bedroom as I think about how she started out with James, his cock inside her mouth. Hopefully she will give me the sort of oral service she gave him. If this is what I can expect after my wife has sex with other men, I'm all for it. Let's get this thing started.

Chapter Seven: Legally Bound

44

"I'm really nervous about this," Karie tells me as she works to clean up a few items from the coffee table in the living room. "I see him every day at work."

"His name's Barry, right?" I ask with a wicked smile on my face. "He's an attorney?"

"Yes," she answers flatly as she turns and looks around the room. "I wish I had thought more about this before I asked him to come over here. We're on lockdown, after all. We shouldn't be letting anyone come to our house if they aren't related to us. The governor says..."

"Honey, they're not going to come to our house and break down the door to see whether Barry is here with us, alright? We're going to be fine."

She shakes her head. "You may feel fine, but I feel like I'm about to throw up, Leyland. He has no clue what's about to happen to him." Karie and I have spent the last couple of days talking about all that has happened between her and the men she has been seeing. All of them have had some crush or desire for my wife and she was happy to help them out with their sexual needs if they could help her as well. Barry, on the other hand, has only approached her very carefully. He hasn't been pushy or overbearing in his attempts to see her. Karie tells me this is because he has heard about the others and wanted to see where his soft advances might get him. Maybe that's true. Either way, he's about to discover that my wife and I are both ready to give him what he desires.

The doorbell rings and Karie stops to look at the door and then at me. "You invited him," I tell her with a chuckle. Though she doesn't like having to do it, my wife makes her way to the front door and opens it to let him in.

"Good afternoon, Karie," the young attorney says as he smiles at her. Then, as if he's been hit hard in the face, his expression changes as he sees me sitting in my recliner.

"Come on in, Barry. It's good to meet you." Karie directs him inside to the sofa where she sits down beside him. His face is a little red as he addresses me.

"Um, hello. Leyland, right?"

I nod my head. "That's right. I would offer you my hand if this virus thing wasn't going around, but I'm sure you understand that."

"I do. We've been asked at work to limit our physical contact with others as well." Barry looks nervously at Karie as he apparently struggles to understand what's going on. After all, he was not told that I would be here this afternoon.

"Would you like anything to drink?" Karie asks him as she smiles.

"I'm good, thank you," he replies nervously.

"So, Barry, what do you do at the firm? My wife has told me that you're a great attorney." I enjoy reminding him that we are sitting together in our living room with my wife.

The young attorney nods his head. "Well, I'm usually involved in civil litigation cases. They're nothing like the criminal law that Karie practices."

"Civil? That means you sue people, right?"

"Or represent those being sued," he replies while smiling briefly. "It keeps me pretty busy."

"I'll bet it does." Karie shoots a sharp look at me as she watches me enjoy toying with the young man. I can't help the way I feel about him, though. I look forward to seeing her have sex with him, but I also have some part of me that's a little annoyed that he has shown up with that expectation in mind.

"Barry, anyway, I wanted to talk to you about the emails that you have been sending me at work, if that's alright." His face turns red as he looks over at Karie. "It's nothing terrible, but I just want to know why you've been emailing me so much."

"Um, so much?" He looks nervously at her and then at me before turning his attention back to my wife.

"Six emails in five days," she replies. "That's a lot of emails asking me to get together with you, right? I'm sorry that I didn't answer you sooner, though. I wasn't sure what to say at first."

Swallowing hard, Barry puts his hands together and begins to fidget a little. "Whatever you think about the emails, just remember that they were thrown together hastily and not really thought through. I don't know why I sent them, to be honest."

"We all know why you sent them," I say with a chuckle. "You're horny and you heard that Karie is putting out."

Leyland!" My wife looks hard at me while shaking her head. She doesn't approve of the way I'm teasing the other man. It could be worse, though. I could be beating his head into the floor instead if I were a very jealous man.

"I'm sorry. I thought that I might break the ice for us. Maybe you can do better in this?" I smile at Karie.

"Maybe I can." She turns and faces the man beside her. "Barry, I'm interested in you too." She leans in and pulls him toward her, locking her lips onto his as her arms wrap around his neck. Though at first he appears to try to refuse the kiss, he is soon kissing my wife back as their tongues move in and out of each other's mouths. After a few seconds of intense lip biting, they separate and Barry looks nervously into my wife's eyes.

"I didn't mean to," he begins before Karie's finger goes to his lip.

"Just sit back and relax." My wife slides into the floor in front of him before she begins to unfasten his pants. For a moment I can see the video from the other day in my mind. Much of this is very similar in the way that Karie took charge in the video to get what she wants from a lover. My cock becomes hard as I watch her open Barry's pants and pull out his hardening cock.

"No, I don't...*shit.*" Barry's hands grip the sofa tightly as my wife puts her lips on his cock and then draws it into her mouth. He closes his eyes for a moment as she gently bobs her head up and down his erect shaft.

"She's good at that," I say to him with a chuckle. "Karie likes giving head. Just let her do her thing, man." I run my hand over the bulge in my own pants. Though I want to pull out my own johnson to jerk off, my wife asked me earlier to avoid doing so with Barry. She fears it might cause him to bolt suddenly if I do.

"I'm not asking for this," he tells us, his eyes wide. "Please don't be upset with me."

Karie lifts her head, a bit of pre-come dripping from her lips. "We're not upset with you, Barry. This is all just for you. Just sit back and relax." She lowers her head again as her hands pull his ball sack out of his pants. My wife massages his robin eggs as she sucks gently on his firm manhood.

"Barry, I want you to come in her mouth when you're ready," I tell him. The look on his face is priceless. "It's okay. I want her to taste your ball juice, alright? Just give her all of your jiss when you feel it's time. Don't hold anything back. Empty your balls into my wife's mouth." The words, even though they come from my mouth, cause me to get very hard. Barry is probably the sort of guy who doesn't get as many blow jobs as he really wants, so there should be a lot of ammo in his sperm gun. He should be able to fill Karie's mouth with his salty DNA quite easily.

"I can't believe this," he huffs as he holds on tightly to the sofa. "Karie's really doing this and you're okay with it?"

"I'm fine for now," I respond. "Just let her do her job. She's not a spitter or a quitter, Barry. Karie likes to swallow everything." I think about the many times in the past that she has given me head. My wife is an expert at doing that sort of thing and there have been plenty of times when I have even pleaded with her for a quick blow job. They have been less frequent as of late than what I would prefer, but I figure that's a part of what Karie has been talking about when she says that our sex life isn't all that great. She's right. Seeing this is giving me plenty of ideas for the future, though.

"Oh, shit, I'm close," I hear Barry say quietly as he puts a hand on Karie's head. "I'm sorry. You don't have to do this. *NAHHHHH!!!*" His face turns red as he begins to launch his seed into my wife's mouth. *"Fuck...FUCK!!!"* Barry's fingers wrap into Karie's hair and he begins to pull at her as he spurts over and over again into the back of her throat.

"Nahhh...ohhhh...uhhhh..." He closes his eyes as he enjoys the way Karie is sucking his cock. Karie gulps several times during the process and with each swallow Barry gets to feel her tongue moving up and around his manhood. I know this technique well, which is why I believe my wife to be among the very best at doing this. Blow jobs are her thing. She loves giving head.

Karie's head eventually comes up after Barry has finished feeding her his genetic soup. "Was that good for you?"

"It was awesome," he says while laying back on the sofa. His face is angled at the ceiling as he considers what has happened just now. The attorney from her law firm has lost his wad in front of me while my wife consumed every single drop of it.

Karie squeezes his shaft and pulls up, causing him to come a little more as his body stiffens. "You have a little more for me." My wife bends down and laps up the excess semen before sitting down on the seat beside him.

"I have to go," Barry tells us as he pushes his wilting stalk back into his pants. "I'm sorry, but I have to go." He gets up from his seat in a hurry and without saying another word he leaves the house through the front door. Karie looks over at me and laughs.

"You know he was scared to death of you, right? You did that to him."

"He was like a deer caught in headlights," I reply. "That's all on him, not me. Still, he did let you do that for him and he came right in front of me." Smiling, I ask, "How did he taste?"

Karie shrugs. "Not bad. I've had better, but not bad."

"Then you need dessert now," I say to my wife as I reach into my pants and pull out my hard phallus. "Here you go."

"Seriously?" I nod my head and Karie shakes hers before she moves toward me and gets on the floor between my legs. She kisses the tip of my dick before sliding it into her mouth.

"Damn, you little vixen," I say with a strained laugh as Karie moves her mouth up and down my shaft. "Fuck, it won't take me long after what I have just seen." She sucks hard on me as she plays with my balls. How the hell Barry held out so long is a mystery to me. I often come within a minute or two of my wife beginning oral sex on me. She's just too good at it for me to be able to refuse to climax quickly. "Fuck."

Karie takes her mouth off me and rubs my cock as she looks into my eyes. "Did you like what you saw with Barry?"

I nod my head. "I was hoping that he would stay around and fuck you, honey." I laugh as my wife smiles at me. She goes back down and my toes point hard inside my shoes. "Dammit, baby. I'll come if you don't stop. *Fuck...*" I take several deep breaths as I prepare to empty into Karie's mouth. Her tongue is so soft and inviting that there's no way I will be able to stop myself.

"Shit, honey...*baby...UHHHH!!!*" I come hard as I feel her tongue on the underside of my long meat stick. *"Ohhhh, baby...uhhhh...ohhhh...."* I wriggle around in my recliner as I feel each powerful ejaculation push my sperm into Karie's waiting mouth. My sexy wife is the best at this and practically everything else having to do with sex. Having another man's spunk in her mouth and stomach makes me want to come harder than I have ever come before.

"Geez...wow." Karie pulls back from my spent cock and then wipes her mouth. There's a lot of semen inside her stomach right now.

"You had a lot to give me," she says with a giggle. "I don't think that you've shot that much into my mouth in a long time, Leyland."

"It's you," I reply. "You drive me nuts, Karie. You always have. But now that you are seeing these other men, it's become more intense for me. A lot more intense."

"Then you understand me, right? I want the other men for the same reason you want to watch me with them. Sex is just so good when there are others involved." She smiles at me. "You know, you should eat my biscuit too. I don't want you to starve, after all."

I smile at her and laugh. "A biscuit it is, then." After standing to my feet, I lead Karie to our bedroom where I can enjoy eating her pussy this morning.

Chapter Eight: Kinky Feelings

Karie giggles as she takes a bite of the large meatball I have made for her with a side of pasta. It's the way my grandmother, a native Italian, made meatballs for us when I was a kid.

"You just like to see me eat balls," Karie says to me with a crooked smile.

"Of course I do," I reply with a laugh. "Especially if you eat *my* balls afterward." We continue to laugh together in between bites of the italian sausage and beef delicacy.

"You really did like what we did, huh? It got you so hard last week, Leyland. I don't think I have seen you that hard in a very long time."

"*You* got me really hard, Karie. Sure, I liked to see what you were doing to him, but you know that you've got a nice way that you give oral sex. You could make a living doing that."

"You would love it if I did that." We both laugh once again as I reach over and put my hand on Karie's lap.

"Would you want to do that again? Maybe to another guy?"

"Oh, really? Another guy? Do you have someone in mind?" my wife asks with a smirk.

I swallow my bite of meatball and pasta noodles before telling her, "I think Ronnie Sykes would appreciate having a little fun with you."

The smile on my wife's face suddenly fades. "You're not serious, right? *Ronnie?* The same guy who is still a little sore about the fact that I chose you over him?"

"You weren't really an item with him back then and I think he understands that now, honey. He's a great guy for you to have a little fun with."

"Leyland, he's a married man. The others so far haven't been married. I've avoided the guys with wives for a reason."

"And I understand that," I reply. "But his wife has decided to go and have sex with someone else behind his back. As a matter of fact, it seems that Michelle might be aware that Ronnie knows about her lover now, but she isn't bothering to try to work things out with him. He deserves the chance to do something like this."

"He thought we were going to get married," she answers. "We didn't do anything but kiss, but Ron was convinced that I was the one for him. It took years to get him to stop sending me letters and email, Leyland. Do we really want to risk getting that going again?"

I shake my head. "You don't like him enough to have sex with him? Do you find him unattractive?"

"No, of course not," she replies. "Ron is actually very attractive. He's really come into his own over the years." A slight grin begins to appear on her lips.

"Then let's do this. He's a nice guy and I think that he would understand that this is a physical thing only. There's no love or romantic relationship that will come of this. If we tell him this upfront, I think Ronnie would be good with the idea of getting to have sex with you."

"He probably would." I can see that Karie is nervous about the idea of having anything like that to do with someone who at one time thought her to be his girlfriend, although she wasn't. My wife knows that men can be fickle at times and then again they can be very unwilling to let go. Ronnie's trouble was that he had decided that he only wanted Karie for his own and that he couldn't let her go very easily. Though it's been over ten years since she chose me as her husband, there is still the possibility that something could blossom inside him that is unintentional on our part.

"Let me talk to him. I think he would really be excited about this. We can make sure that he understands the boundaries, okay? What do you say? Can I call him?"

"Now?" A nervous laugh comes from Karie's lips. "Seriously?"

"We could do it now and get things rolling along. Of course, if he acts a little too weird, we can hang up and just move on to someone else. What do you think?" I smile at Karie as I try to put her a little more at ease.

She sighs. "Alright, let's do it. You can call him up and put him on speaker phone so that I can hear what he says."

"Do you want to say something to him too?" I ask as I pull my cell phone out of my shirt pocket.

"I don't know. I'll stay quiet unless I feel like I need to say something," she replies as she sits back in her chair. Karie watches as I find Ronnie's phone number and press the screen to call it before laying the phone down on the table between us. As he answers, I press the speaker button on my phone so that we can both hear him.

"Hello?"

"Hey, Ronnie, this is Leyland," I reply. "I thought that I would call and see how things are going with you."

"Well, things are okay," he answers questioningly. "And how about for you?"

"I'm good," I say as I smile at Karie next to me. She covers her mouth as her face turns red. "What's up?"

"Are you still in that place in D.C.?"

There's a short silence on the other end of the line before he answers me. "I'm still here. I don't know when I'll be able to go home."

"Well, what are you doing with your free time, then? Are you talking to Michelle at all?"

Ronnie sighs. "She's doing what she wants to do while I'm away. I can't stop her."

"Or you won't," I press him. I realize that I'm jabbing at the guy, but I want him to begin to think about how he's not had access to his wife's pussy in a long time. Maybe I can get him horny enough to actually want Karie.

"I can't help what's going on with her."

"You can help yourself," I tell him. As I look at my wife, I ask, "How would you like to come to our house and spend some quality time with Karie?" Goosebumps rise along the back of my neck.

"Um, what?"

I clear my throat. "Come to my house. Karie is willing to help you with the things that Michelle isn't helping you with right now." There's another long silence as Ronnie is apparently processing the offer. What could he be thinking right now other than that I am out of my mind in offering such a thing?

"Are you trying to be an ass?" Ronnie asks with a growl.

"He's being serious," My wife suddenly chimes in. Her face is red as she talks to the man on the other end of the line.

"Karie?" There's genuine surprise in the sound of his voice.

"We want you to come over, Ron. I want you to come over."

"But..." He stops for a moment and I wonder whether we have lost him on the other end. However, after a few seconds more, Ronnie asks, "Why?"

"Because we are going to choose someone to invite to our home for this and we want that someone to be you. What your wife has done to you isn't fair and we want to help you out," I reply. It's as simple as that, though I get why he is so doubtful of what he's being offered.

"Come see us," Karie tells him. "I want to see you. Maybe back when we dated we should have gone to bed together. I'll make it up to you if you come to see us. I promise." My cock gets hard as I watch my wife work her magic on Ronnie. If he agrees to this, it will only be because she knows how to get to him to convince him to come see her.

"I just can't believe this. I don't know."

"Come see us," I say again. "It will be worth your while. Anything goes while you're here."

"I'm not bisexual," he replies abruptly.

"I know. Neither am I. But, I will want to watch. That's my price for letting you have sex with my wife. If you're okay with that, I'm good with you having sex with Karie."

"What do you say?" Karie asks. "Will you come to our house to spend some time with me?" Her face continues to burn red as my wife becomes more persistent. She knows that we're close to getting Ronnie to agree to come see us.

Ronnie sighs on the phone before answering, "I will come over if that's really what you want. Karie, are you sure that you want me to be with you in that way?"

"Of course I do," she replies. "I'm already wet with anticipation." She smiles at me and winks as she reaches into her pants and plays with her clit. "Come see me, Ron. I want you so badly."

"Shit, honey," I say quietly as I attempt to move my hard shaft around inside my pants.

"Okay," he says quietly. "When would you like me to come by?"

"Friday," I answer. "Just bring yourself and we'll have drinks first, okay? How does that sound to you?"

"It sounds great." Ronne seems happier now than he did before. I'm sure he will probably sit back and jerk himself off after he hangs up the phone. After all, that's what any red-blooded man would do after talking to my wife about having sex with her.

"We'll see you Friday at about seven in the evening." Karie smiles at me and for a second time winks. "I can't wait, Ron."

"I look forward to it too." Ronne hangs up his phone and then I do the same with mine. We've done it. Karie and I have convinced him that he should come over to see her and to have sex with my beautiful wife.

"Do you think he'll change his mind?" she asks.

"Nah," I reply. "Ronnie is a pretty straight shooter when it comes to what he says he will or will not do. I think he'll be here on Friday at seven o'clock sharp."

Karie nods her head. "Do you think I poured it on a little too thick? I think that maybe I sounded a little too desperate. Am I desperate?" My wife smiles as she cocks up one eyebrow.

"Well, you're probably a *little* desperate. I mean, that's what has driven you to a small degree to do what you have been doing, right? You feel desperate and so you are willing to do whatever is necessary to get what you need. Ronnie is in a similar situation."

"His wife sucks," Karie says with a grimace.

"Probably not," I joke as I look sideways at her. My wife laughs while shaking her head. "I know that's a little crude. Still, Michelle is a real bitch for ignoring her husband for another man. He's a nice guy and she's plunged a knife into his heart."

"She's an asshole for having him stay away just so that she could enjoy the company of other men."

"But, isn't that what you did as well?" The question on my part isn't meant to be a critique of what has been going on with Karie at our home while I have been away. Instead, it's an honest analysis of two women and what they are doing to pursue their sexual desires.

"I didn't try to keep you away. I knew that you were being kept away by the pandemic concerns. Leyland, I hope you think better of me than that. Yes, I've had sex with other men, but I didn't mean to hurt you. I would have never been so obvious as to make you uncomfortable about coming home."

"I guess you're right," I say as I nod my head. I reach over and take Karie's hand into mine as I add, "I love you. You do know that, right?"

"I know. Hopefully you see that I love you more than anything else, too. Remember, all that has happened between me and the others has been just for the physical needs I have had for a while. There was never an emotional connection with any of them. You know that, right?"

"Yeah, I do."

Karie looks into my eyes and adds, "I haven't been able to see a movie with you in a long time. What are we going to do about that?"

"Oh, I don't know. We have Hulu and Netflix. Should we find something and sit back on the sofa with each other?"

My wife smiles as she gets up from her chair at the table. "The dishes can wait. Let's go watch a movie." I stand to my feet and allow Karie to lead me to the living room. Date nights for us are often on the sofa in our living room. The nice thing about them is that after the movie we sometimes end up going to our bedroom to have a little fun. Hopefully that's where this will be heading very soon.

Chapter Nine: Mutually Desired

"Come in," I say to the other man as I look at him from across the threshold of our front door. Ronnie nods his head and walks into the foyer before I lead him into the living room and then the dining room. "Karie will be right with us." I motion toward a chair at the end of the dining room table and he has a seat. Reaching for a bottle of wine, I ask, "Do you like Cabernet?"

"Yeah, I like it," he replies. Ronnis is obviously nervous as I open the bottle and pour us each a glass of wine. I pass one of the glasses to him and watch as he takes a sip of it. "It's very good," he tells me with a slight smile on his face. His eyes look around the dining room as he takes a second drink.

"She's getting ready and then she will bring the food in here. It was her idea what to cook for this evening. I hope you like truffles."

Ronnie nods his head. "I've only had them once, but I liked them. I didn't know Karie could cook."

I laugh. "Well, back in college she definitely couldn't. After we got married, I did the lion's share of it for the two of us. Since then, she's made it a point to try to become better than me at it. She still has a long way to go." We both laugh as Karie walks into the dining room. Ronnie almost spits out a sip of wine in his mouth when he sees her.

"I heard that, Leyland. I think my truffles and gravy is much better than your roast duck."

"I don't think so," I joke with her. Ronnie's eyes are affixed on my wife's body which is easy to see through the thin negligee that she is wearing. My cock gets hard as I think about what must be going through his mind at this moment. Though he dated her at one time, he's never seen her naked.

"Where's my glass?" Karie smiles at me as she ignores Ronnie's lustful gaze. It's a tactic that she sometimes uses on me to get me worked up before sex. It seems to be working very well on our guest.

"Oh, here you go." I pour my wife a glass of wine and hand it to her. Karie's dark pink nipples are easy to see through the fabric and I get the feeling that Ronnie is studying every part of those and the rest of her body.

"Let's have a seat," I say to her as I nod my head toward where she will be seated beside Ronnie. Karie sits down and I do as well before she begins to dole out servings of truffles with gravy.

"I've never had this as a standalone dish," the diplomatic aide remarks as he looks at the dark fungus. "I've had it served with chicken."

"It's really good this way too," Karie replies. At this point, I believe it would be best for me to simply sit back and watch them together. "I have a sister who is a chef and she taught me to make this." My wife takes a quick sip of her wine as she turns more toward him. Her nipples are pressed against the thin material, leaving nothing to the imagination as she addresses him.

Ronnie nods his head and takes a bite of his food. "It is good," he says with a smile after swallowing the morsel.

"Of course it's good. But only with gravy," Karie replies. "Everything's better with gravy." My wife opens the negligee to expose her beautiful breasts. Ronnie sits still and watches as he chews a second bite of his food. She then takes the gravy ladle and puts a smear of the dark gravy on both nipples. "Oh, dear. It seems I've made a mess."

"Holy shit," I say under my breath as I reach down to move my hardening manhood around. There was nothing about what she said earlier that indicated to me that Karie would be doing anything like this. Nothing.

"Um..." Ronnie is unsure what he should do. So, Karie gets up from her seat and walks over to him.

"Help me clean these off," she tells him with a seductive smile. Our guest reaches for his napkin, but she puts her hand down to stop him.

"Not that way. Those are good napkins that might stain with this much gravy. Can't you get it off my breasts without wiping them off?" Karie smiles mischievously at Ronnie as she gets closer to him. He finally understands what she wants and moves closer so that he can press his lips to one of her nipples. "There you go." My wife closes her eyes as he cleans each nipple very well with his mouth.

"Tastes good, huh?" I say as I nod my head at him. "Enjoy that, Ronnie. She made it just for you." He spends a couple of minutes moving from one nipple to the other, even continuing to lick and suck at them after the gravy has disappeared. It seems that he's enjoying himself a great deal as he licks my wife's taut mammary glands.

"Oh, Ron," she moans as she puts her hands behind his head to pull him closer to her. "Suck them hard for me. Fuck." Karie bites her bottom lip as she enjoys the way he nips and nibbles at her chest. There is no doubt now what she wants or that he wants to give it to her. They are now two lovers in time with each other.

"Karie," Ronnie says to her as he pulls her head down to his and kisses her hard. He has wanted my wife for more than ten years and now he has her. All of her attention is on him and all of his is on her as they move their hands around to become familiar with each other's bodies. Ronnie's fingers find her wet muff and begin to dig into her as she grinds around on them.

"Oh, fuck, stop," Karie says as she pushes herself back from him. It seems at first that she's had enough of Ronnie and is ready to stop. However, she sits down on the end of the table in front of Ronnie and pushes his plate away as she says, "I've got gravy on my pussy, Ron. Clean it up for me, okay?" She lies back so that he can see her soft, wet muff. Karie has begun to cream herself with her vaginal juices and she wants him to help her take care of this mess as well.

"I can't believe you're letting me do this," he tells her as he sniffs her snapper. Then, as if he doesn't need permission to do so, Ronnie buries his face into her nethers and begins to lick and lap at my wife's hard clitoris and soft labia.

"Oh, shit, Ron," Karie squeals as she grinds her pussy into his wet face. "Oh, shit."

"Put your tongue inside her pussy," I say as I get up and go to where he is having his dessert. "There you go. Inside her. See how sweet she is?" Ronnie turns his attention to my wife's swollen clit and begins to suck on it, causing her to arch her back with every lap.

"Fuck, you're driving me crazy, Ron," she groans as she puts her feet on his shoulders. "Oh, you're really driving me crazy. Fuck..." Karie puts her hands on his head, weaving her fingers into Ronnie's hair as he enjoys her musky flavor. I'm a little jealous of him, but not because he is with my wife right now. I'm jealous because I would love to be the one tasting her sweet pussy.

"I need you," he says to her as he pulls back and stands to his feet. Ronnie drops his pants and briefs before rubbing his hard cock against her wet muffin. He shudders as he draws it up Karie's wet slit, her hard clit getting the majority of the attention. "I have to fuck you, Karie. I've always wished that I had fucked you back then." He presses the large head of his penis against her wet hole and then pushes it into her. My wife's petite body bucks a little as he gets very deep inside her.

"Fuck, that's my cervix," she tells him as he pushes her legs back and begins to thrust in and out of her.

"Fuck her hard," I plead with Ronnie as my wife winces. "Come inside her pussy."

"Ronnie..." He's sliding against Karie's G-spot as he saws in and out of her tight hole. My wife purses her lips and holds onto the edge of the dining room table as he keeps stimulating her orgasmic center.

"So tight," he mutters as he enjoys the feeling of her soft, wet vagina wrapped around his pulsating cock. I watch as her pussy lips cling to the sides of his manhood while he moves in and out of her. Karie's toes begin to point as she reaches up and plays with her own perky nipples.

"Holy fuck, baby," she squeals as she turns red in the face. "I'm going to come soon."

"Me too," Ronnie replies. "I want to come inside you, Karie. Can I come inside you? Please don't make me pull out just before I come."

My wife opens her eyes. "Come inside me, sweetie. Come really hard." She closes her eyes again as her back arches steeply. "Oh, Leyland, this is so good. Thank you for letting me...*UHHHHHHH!!!*" Karie begins to come hard as she squirts a little of her pussy juices onto Ronnie's thrusting cock. *"Ohhhh!!! AHHHHH!!! Ronnie...RONNIE!!!"* Her pelvis rocks along with him as he moves faster and faster inside my wife. My own cock is hard and pre-coming inside my pants as I watch the two of them together.

"KARIEEEE!!!" Ronnie loses his wad as he pushes her legs further back and wedges his cock deep inside her tight pussy. *"GAHHHH!!! FUCK!!! OHHHH..."* The dining room table is moving so hard that I begin to worry that the legs might give out. I go to the other end and use my body to brace it so that the two of them can continue to enjoy each other without this concern. *"NAHHHH!!!"*

Their bodies continue to rock for a minute or so longer until the two of them come down from their orgasm together. Karie smiles at Ronnie as he pulls out of her and sits down in a chair nearby. His eyes focus on the thick white cream that is running out of my wife and onto the table beneath her.

"You two were really into that, huh?" I say with a laugh. "I think the neighbor might have heard you."

"Trina?" my wife says with a scoff. "She can go fuck someone else for all I care. I'm tired of worrying about her and what she's seen or thought she's seen. Screw her."

Ronnie looks from Karie to me and then back again. "I hope that was alright. I'm a little rusty and I was very nervous when I got here."

"That's understandable," I tell him. "It's all good, though. Right, honey?"

"Very good." Karie sits up on the table and then stands on the floor. She pulls Ronnie close to her and gives him a long, hard kiss. He returns it in kind and then smiles at her.

"Is it possible that we could do this again in the near future?"

"Maybe," Karie answers him. "We'll see how things go, Ron. Just give me some time to think things over." She kisses him again before leaving the dining room to take a shower in the master suite.

After a quiet moment in the dining room, Ronnie says to me, "Thanks for letting this happen. I really did need something to help me deal with what Michelle is doing."

Nodding my head, I reply, "I know you did. Look, if she's okay with doing this again, I am too. I know that Michelle isn't really taking care of things with you the way that she should. Have you tried to talk to her at all?"

Ronnie shakes his head. "There's no talking to my wife. She knows that I know about her lover and she's refused to answer my text messages and phone calls. I think things are probably over for us." He reaches down and picks up his pants and underwear to put them back on.

"That sucks, man. I'll talk to Karie, alright? I'll bet I can warm her up to doing this again with you. I mean, she really seemed to like this."

"So did I." I watch as Ronnie gets dressed and then I see him to the door. None of us care to finish our dinner tonight. After all, Ronnie has already had his dessert. Truffles just can't compare to that.

Chapter Ten: The Needs of the Two

Karie and I sit out on our back patio late on a Saturday afternoon as we enjoy some cold lemonade. It's been some time since we have made the refreshing drink for ourselves. Having so much time at home with the pandemic raging across the country has given us the opportunity to do a lot of things that we haven't done in a while.

"He was pretty good," my wife says to me as she looks out over the back yard. "Ronnie knew what he was doing when he went down on me. What the hell is wrong with his wife, though?"

I chuckle. "She's a horny woman who wants more than just a nice bit of cunnilingus, I guess. Ronne did really go after you with his mouth. He wasn't worried about me being right next to the two of you at all."

"He's good." Karie smiles to herself as she runs her fingers across her chest. She has decided to sit outside in a two-piece bikini to enjoy the warm afternoon.

"So, do you want to do that with him again?"

"With Ron?" She looks over at me and I nod. "Yeah, I would like to give him a nice blow job next time. I planned to do that at dinner the other night, but then things just started up and I couldn't stop what was happening."

"I noticed." Smiling, I ask, "And what about other men? Do you want to keep that up as well? You seem to have calmed down a little, but you hid it from me really well in the beginning. I know better than to underestimate your desires now."

Karie nods her head. "If it's alright with you, I would like to see other men. I don't mind if you watch me with them if you let me keep doing that."

"I think that would be fine." I look over at where our neighbor Trina is sitting in her backyard. She too has decided to wear a skimpy bikini while enjoying the waning sunlight.

"And you would like to have a shot at her in bed, huh?" Karie jokes as she looks from Trina to me.

"What? No, of course not," I reply emphatically. "She's at least ten years older than me, honey."

"She's also very hot." Karie smiles as she looks back over at our neighbor. "I think Trina has a thing for you anyway, Leyland. You're practically the only one she will talk to in the neighborhood. She won't hardly give me the time of day."

"That's because you rarely come out here, Karie. When you do, it's to sit and read a book. Trina isn't going to call over to you and try to start a conversation. She probably feels like you are ignoring her anyway."

"I am," Karie laughs. "She's a nosy neighbor, Ley. I honestly don't like that woman very much. But I can see why you might enjoy getting to know her better."

"At least she told me about you and your friends."

"My friends," my wife scoffs. "Trina wasn't even sure what was going on over here. She thought it was all for my work. She told you that when you spoke to her about it, right? Anyway, she keeps an eye on everything we do over here. Nothing is sacred around the neighborhood with her. She'll share all of our secrets with anyone willing to listen at all.

"Maybe she would." I take a sip of my own lemonade.

"You can have her," Karie says to me again. "I want to watch when it happens, but you can have her. She's willing to fuck you, Leyland. I would swear to that."

"Honey." I look over and can see that I'm wasting my time arguing with her. When my wife gets something into her head, she rarely lets it go.

"Just think about it, Leyland. Let me know if you want to do it and we'll get things set up. Trina would be thrilled about it. With her husband gone, she probably hasn't had much attention like that in a long time. Besides, I want to see how you would behave with another woman." Karie smiles wickedly as she gets up from her seat. "I need a refill. What about you?"

"I've still got plenty," I tell her before watching Karie make her way into the house. I look over at the older woman next door and think about what my wife has just said. Would Trina want to have sex with me? Of all the times that we've spoken to each other, I don't recall a single time when she has made it clear that she's attracted to me. Though I think Karie might be reading far too much into how Trina feels about me, I would seriously consider fucking her if given the chance. My cock is almost always a little stiff when I talk to her.

Trina waves at me from her yard and I nod my head back at her while raising my glass. I smile at her as I look over at her. I want the older woman, but I'm not so certain that she wants me. The neighbor gets up from her seat and makes her way to the hedge row that separates our lawns. Once she gets there, she says to me, "You know, if you ever want to come over and talk for a while, Leyland, I'm here for you." The woman then winks before pulling up her top to reveal her perfectly round breasts to me. My jaw drops as she shakes them a little and then covers them back up. Trina turns back around and walks into her house to leave me to my thoughts after showering my eyes with her beautiful body.

"Fuck," I say quietly to myself. "Fuck."

THE END

Don't miss out!

Visit the website below and you can sign up to receive emails whenever Karly Violet publishes a new book. There's no charge and no obligation.

https://books2read.com/r/B-A-GIXE-HDVOB

BOOKS 2 READ

Connecting independent readers to independent writers.

About the Author

Sign up to my mailing list to receive the two free epilogues for 'A Hotwife Adventure' and 'Hotwife Training' and to stay up to date on all of my latest releases! http://eepurl.com/c3ICWf Sign up to my Patreon account and receive exclusive Hotwife stories every month and sexy scenes every week! https://www.patreon.com/karlyviolet

Read more at https://www.patreon.com/karlyviolet.

About the Publisher

9 798201 844332